Spooky Hour

For Rosa and Trudi – T.M.

For Sian and Laura

and special thanks for the Goldy magic – G.P.R.

Text copyright © 2003 by Tony Mitton
Illustrations copyright © 2003 by Guy Parker-Rees
First published in Great Britain in 2003 by Orchard Books London.

Library of Congress Cataloging-in-Publication Data available
ISBN 0-439-60373-0

10 9 8 7 6 5 4 3 2 1   04 05 06 07 08
First Scholastic edition, August 2004
Printed in Hong Kong

Spooky Hour

BY TONY MITTON

Illustrated by
GUY PARKER-REES

ORCHARD BOOKS / NEW YORK
An Imprint of Scholastic Inc.

BONG! goes the bell in the rickety tower,
Twelve times... that means it's Spooky Hour.

Listen! Hush! Oooh, what's that sound?
The midnight spooks are coming 'round.

Then off they zoom on broomsticks, "Wheeeeeee!"

Out of the darkness, what's this here?

Ten funny, floaty ghosts appear,

Swirling, whirling, singing, "Whooooooo!

Watch out, witches. We're after youoooooooo!"

Nine skeletons dance by, clickety clack.
Their snapping teeth go snickety snack.

At the edge of the trees, tu-whit tu-whoo,
Eight spooky owls hoot, "We'll come, too."

Sneaking closer now, what's this?

Prowling, yowling, scowling – Hisssss!

Leaping high and creeping low,

Seven scary cats with eyes that glow!

From deep in the woods comes a rumbling sound,

As **six** trolls tromp the **grumbling** ground.

And what's that scuttling?

Better be wary...

Five
big
spiders,
fat
and
hairy.

Shadows leap as your heart beats quicker.
Through the trees comes a splutter-and-flicker.

Four wizards, holding lanterns bright,
Go by in dancing candlelight.

Beside the gate to the castle yard,
Three suits of armor stand on guard.

A noise comes swirling down the stair.

Let's go on up. Oh, do we dare?

"Cackle cackle...tee-hee-hee..."

I wonder who that is?

Let's see...

"Surp

Standing there with

rise!"

two big grins,
Are Mitch and Titch,
the witchy twins.

And what's this here?
Oh me, oh my!
It's...

ONE GI
PUMPKI

Then Mitch says, "Come on, everyone.
Let's have some scary party fun!"

They hide away
in funny places,
Then pop out:

BOO!

with spooky faces.

They leap and swirl,
they howl and shriek,
As they play at screechy
hide-and-seek.

But even spooks can have enough,
And in the end, they're out of puff.

Then home they go to snuggly beds.